Little Naomi, Little Chick

Little Naomi, Little Chick

Written by

Avirama Golan

Illustrated by

Raaya Karas

Translated from the Hebrew by Annette Appel

Eerdmans Books for Young Readers

Grand Rapids, Michigan • Cambridge, U.K.

To Naomi, of course.
— **A. G.**

Dedicated with love to my parents,

who have stood by me ever since I was a little chick.
— *R. K.*

Good morning!

Little Naomi jumps out of bed.

She gets ready for the day ahead.

She brushes her teeth

and washes her face,

eats breakfast

and makes sure her schoolbag's in place.

She gives Little Bear a hug.

She kisses Mommy

and gives Daddy's hand a tug.

Little Naomi is ready to go!

Off to preschool, with Daddy in tow.

But **not** Little Chick.

At school
Little Naomi meets all her friends —
Sofia, Max, and Emma,
Lily, Daniel, and Ella.
Mrs. Kim, her teacher, greets them all
with a big hello.
Naomi puts her backpack away,
says good-bye to Daddy, and goes to play.

But **not** Little Chick.

Naomi plays with blocks

and builds a tower,

feeds the dolls

and picks some flowers.

She rolls around,

and jumps up and down.

She bakes some mud pies

and flops on the ground.

But **not** Little Chick.

Story time!
Naomi hears a story about a bunny
who lost his tail and thought it was funny.
Then she makes a picture
with all of her paints —
pink and green,
yellow and blue.
Red and brown,
and purple too.

But **not** Little Chick.

The bell rings.

It's time for lunch!

Is this for me?

No, it's for Naomi!

Meatballs and rice.

A tomato, one slice.

A green pickle to crunch.

Sweet strawberries to munch.

Naomi picks up her spoon and eats all by herself.

She finishes her lunch without any help.

But **not** Little Chick.

Next it's time to wash up
and roll out the mats.
Everyone gets ready
for the afternoon nap.
Soon all are sleeping,
sound as can be —
Lily, Sofia, Ella, and Max,
Emma, Daniel, and Naomi.

But **not** Little Chick.

Who is the first to awake at midday?
Naomi, of course.
She runs out to play.
And who is that walking
along the way?
It's Mommy, sweet Mommy —
she's off work for the day.
A hug!
A kiss!
Another kiss!

Naomi gets her backpack
and says bye to her friends.
She heads home with Mommy,
walking hand in hand.

But **not** Little Chick.

On the way home, Mommy stops
at the grocery store.
She buys bread, cheese, and eggs,
butter and more.
Naomi helps Mommy load the cart.
She already knows the list by heart.

But **not** Little Chick.

At the playground,
Naomi climbs and slides,
swings and glides.
Behind the trees
the sun is low,
and Naomi knows
it's time to go.

But **not** Little Chick.

Daddy's home.
Dinner time!

Now what could that be?
A fish called Naomi?
No.
A dolphin? A whale?
A duck with a tail?

No, no, no.
Naomi is taking a bath
with a splish and a splash.
She washes her tummy and neck,
her bottom and back.

All clean!
Daddy gets a fluffy towel
to dry Naomi off.
She puts on her bunny pajamas
and gets into bed with a hop.

But **not** Little Chick.

Good night!

Mommy sings two lullabies.

Shh ... It's late.

Now go to sleep.

Naomi pulls the blanket tight.

She is not alone tonight.

Little Bear rests by her side.

Naomi yawns and closes her eyes.

And Little Chick?

What about Little Chick?

Yes, **yes**.

Little Chick too snuggles in for the night.

Shh ... Please don't make a peep.

Little Chick is fast asleep.

Text © 2012 Avirama Golan
Illustrations © 2012 Raaya Karas
English language translation © 2012 Kinneret Zmora-Bitan Publishing
Published by arrangement with Kinneret Zmora-Bitan Publishing,
Or Yehuda, Israel

Original Title: Little Naomi, Little Chick

Published in 2013 by Eerdmans Books for Young Readers,
an imprint of Wm. B. Eerdmans Publishing Co.
2140 Oak Industrial Dr. NE
Grand Rapids, Michigan 49505
P.O. Box 163, Cambridge CB3 9PU U.K.

www.eerdmans.com/youngreaders

Manufactured at Tien Wah Press in Malaysia
in March 2013, first printing

19 18 17 16 15 14 13   9 8 7 6 5 4 3 2 1

Library of Congress Cataloging-in-Publication Data

Golan, Avirama.
Little Naomi, Little Chick / by Avirama Golan;
illustrated by Raaya Karas.
pages cm
Summary: Little Naomi has a fun and busy day at preschool and with
her family, while Little Chick has a busy, fun day on the farm.
ISBN 978-0-8028-5427-8
[1. Nursery schools — Fiction. 2. Schools — Fiction.
3. Chickens — Fiction. 4. Animals — Infancy — Fiction.
5. Farm life — Fiction.] I. Karas, Raaya, illustrator. II. Title.
PZ7.G5612Lit 2013
[E] — dc23
2013000492

The illustrations were rendered in crayon and pencil.
The display type was set in Sweet Pea.
The text type was set in Gil Sans.